The Veil of Silence

Michael Davies

ISBN: 978-1-916732-49-0

Published By: -

i2i

P U B L I S H I N G

i2i Publishing. Manchester.
www.i2ipublishing.co.uk

Contents

The Veil of Silence

Chapter 1: The Anatomy of a Killer

Thomas Greene was born in the quiet, unremarkable town of Dartley, nestled in the rolling hills of southern England. It was a place where life moved slowly, and the people who lived there seemed to age with the brickwork of the ancient, terraced houses that lined the narrow streets. Dartley was not known for much — an old cathedral, a weekly market, and a scattering of pubs that had seen better days. For most, it was a place to settle down, raise a family, and live out a simple, predictable life.

Thomas's parents, Elaine and Richard Greene, were as ordinary as the town they inhabited. His father was a mechanic who spent long hours in a dimly lit garage, while his mother worked part-time as a secretary at the local council office. They were quiet people, content with their routine, and they raised Thomas to be the same. There were no outbursts of emotion in the Greene household, no heated arguments or moments of tenderness. It was a house of silence, where the ticking of the old clock in the living room often felt like the loudest sound.

As a child, Thomas was withdrawn and solitary. He was never the kind of boy who ran through the fields or played with other children in the park. Instead, he spent most of his time indoors, quietly observing the world around him. He was the type of child who could sit for hours, staring out of the window, watching the birds in the garden or the occasional car pass by. His parents, who were not overly affectionate, seemed content with his behaviour. As long as he wasn't causing trouble, they didn't pay much attention to what he did.

From a young age, Thomas had an unusual fascination with the concept of life and death. He would sit in his room for hours, reading books about anatomy, studying diagrams of the human body with a level of focus that was almost unnerving. He was particularly drawn to the workings of the heart and brain, organs that he believed held the secrets of existence. When other children were playing video games or watching cartoons, Thomas was poring over medical textbooks he had borrowed from the town's small library.

At school, Thomas was the boy who went unnoticed. He had no friends to speak of, and he preferred it that way. His teachers described him as polite but distant, a student who did what was required without drawing attention to himself. He excelled in science, particularly biology, but showed little interest in any other subject. The other children found him odd, but he wasn't bullied. He simply wasn't memorable enough to warrant anyone's attention.

As he grew older, Thomas's fascination with the human body deepened. While most teenagers were preoccupied with fitting in or finding their place in the world, Thomas spent his time exploring the woods and fields around Dartley, collecting small animals—frogs, birds, and sometimes even stray cats. He would take them back to an old shed behind his parents' house, where he dissected them with the same careful precision he had seen in his textbooks.

He kept meticulous notes on their anatomy, observing the differences between life and death with a detached curiosity.

By the time Thomas reached his late teens, his parents had largely given up trying to connect with him. They chalked his behaviour up to introversion and perhaps a little eccentricity, but they weren't concerned. Thomas had never caused trouble, never asked for anything, and never broke the rules. He was the kind of son who could disappear into his room for hours, and no one would notice.

When he turned eighteen, Thomas left Dartley to attend university in London. He enrolled in a biomedical sciences program, where he could immerse himself fully in the study of the human body. The city was overwhelming at first — the noise, the crowds, the ceaseless motion — but Thomas quickly adapted. He found solace in the anonymity that London offered. Here, he was just another face in the crowd, unnoticed and unremarkable.

At university, Thomas excelled in his studies. His professors recognized his potential and praised his meticulous attention to detail, though they often noted his lack of engagement with his peers. Thomas was content to remain on the fringes, spending his free time in the lab, dissecting cadavers and studying the intricacies of human tissue. He developed a particular interest in neurology, fascinated by the brain's control over the body, and the delicate balance between consciousness and unconsciousness.

During his time at university, Thomas's curiosity about the boundary between life and death took on a darker edge. The more he studied, the more he became obsessed with the idea of control — how the body could be manipulated, how life could be extended or snuffed out with the right knowledge and tools. He began to see his experiments as more than academic exercises. They became personal.

After completing his degree, Thomas decided against pursuing a traditional medical career. Instead, he took a job as a hospital support worker in a smaller hospital on the outskirts of London. It was a position that allowed him to remain close to the operating theatres, where he could watch surgeries and observe the surgeons at work, but without the responsibility of making decisions about patients' lives. It was the perfect position for someone who wanted to stay in the background, unnoticed.

For several years, Thomas worked quietly in the hospital, blending into the fabric of the institution. He was efficient, reliable, and never caused any trouble. His colleagues regarded him as a bit of a loner, but he did his job well, and that was all that mattered. He spent most of his time cleaning up after surgeries, preparing the operating rooms, and occasionally assisting the nurses and doctors with minor tasks.

Outside of work, Thomas's life was a void. He lived alone in a small, drab apartment, devoid of personal touches or decorations. His interactions with others were minimal, limited to the occasional polite exchange with his neighbours or coworkers. His evenings were spent reading medical journals, watching surgical videos, His fascination with the boundary between life and death had grown into something darker — an obsession with control.

Chapter 2: The Quiet Observer

That night at work the hum of fluorescent lights filled the sterile corridor as Thomas wheeled the empty gurney back to the operating theatre. It was nearly midnight, and the hospital had quieted down, save for the occasional muffled page over the intercom. He liked this time of night – the stillness, the order. It was in the silence that Thomas could think.

He moved with purpose, his footsteps soft on the polished linoleum floor. As a support worker, Thomas had seen it all – the blood, the gore, the miraculous moments when a patient's life was saved, and the solemn moments when it wasn't. But none of that disturbed him. In fact, it fascinated him.

He entered Operating Theatre 5, the scene of the day's final surgery. The room was empty now, save for the remnants of the procedure. Surgical tools gleamed under the overhead lights, and the scent of antiseptic lingered in the air. Thomas paused for a moment, surveying the space. To most, it would look like a place of healing. To him, it was a stage – a place where the line between life and death was blurred.

On the counter, just within reach, was a vial of propofol. The clear liquid glistened inside the glass, unassuming yet so powerful. It was the drug of choice for inducing unconsciousness, a tool for the anaesthetists. But to Thomas, it was something more. It was control.

He reached out, his hand trembling slightly, and pocketed the vial. It wasn't the first time. He knew how to cover his tracks, how to take just enough so that it wouldn't be noticed. No one would miss this small amount. The hospital was busy, chaotic. People made mistakes.

As he left the theatre and made his way out into the cool night air, Thomas's mind raced. The vial felt heavy in his pocket, a promise of things to come. He walked down the darkened street, his eyes scanning the empty sidewalks. Somewhere out there, someone was waiting for him—they just didn't know it yet.

Chapter 3: The First Cut

The streetlights cast long shadows across the quiet alley as Thomas Greene made his way through the city. It had become routine for him, these late-night walks, where the world seemed to hold its breath, and he could slip between the cracks, unnoticed. He liked the stillness of the night, the way the darkness cloaked him like a shroud. No one was awake to see him—no one to ask questions.

He passed a diner, its neon sign flickering in the distance, and kept walking until the sidewalks became narrower, more deserted. The vial in his pocket weighed heavier with each step, a reminder of what he had set out to do. He told himself it was still curiosity that drove him, a scientific inquiry into the boundaries of consciousness. But deep down, Thomas knew the truth. He craved the power.

Ahead, he saw her.

She was walking alone, her head down, a bag slung over one shoulder. She was young, maybe in her twenties, dressed in a coat too light for the chill in the air. Her footsteps echoed softly in the night, the rhythm steady and unaware. She wasn't paying attention to him, but Thomas noticed everything about her—the way she carried herself, the slight limp in her gait, the faint puff of breath in the cold air.

He followed her, keeping his distance, his mind working through the plan he had perfected. It wasn't the first time he'd done this—stolen glances at potential victims, sizing them up, deciding whether they were worth the effort. But this time, something was different. Tonight, he was ready.

As she turned down an even quieter street, Thomas quickened his pace. His heart raced, not from fear, but from anticipation. He felt alive in these moments, more so than he ever had in the sterile world of the hospital. In the operating theatre, he was an observer, a silent witness to the delicate dance between life and death. But here, outside the bounds of morality, he was in control.

His hand slid into his pocket, his fingers brushing the cool glass of the vial. The needle was ready, prepped in his other pocket. He had studied the dosage carefully, tested it enough times to know exactly how much would knock someone out without causing any permanent damage — at least, not yet. It had to be precise. That was the difference between an artist and a butcher, after all.

She slowed, stopping to check something on her phone. Her fingers tapped away at the screen, unaware of the predator stalking her. Thomas closed the distance in a few long strides, his hand already reaching for her before she could react.

The cloth, soaked in the anaesthetic mixture, pressed firmly over her mouth. Her eyes went wide with shock, and for a split second, she struggled — her hands flailing against his chest — but it was too late. He held her tightly, his heart pounding in sync with the pulse beneath his fingers. The anaesthetic worked quickly, just as it had in the animals he'd practiced on. Within moments, her body went limp, the fight drained from her as her eyelids fluttered and closed.

Thomas let her slide to the ground, his breath ragged in the cold night air. He stood over her for a moment, staring down at her unconscious form, the first of many. The street was empty, quiet, and the world seemed to shrink around him as if nothing else existed but him and her. He felt a rush of exhilaration. There was no guilt, no hesitation—just the cold, clinical precision of a surgeon about to make the first cut.

Carefully, he hoisted her body over his shoulder, moving with a surprising strength that belied his slender frame. He had planned for this. In the abandoned warehouse not far from here, there was a space he had prepared, a place where no one would find her. It wasn't much, just a cold, forgotten room with a table in the center and a few tools laid out neatly on a tray. But it was enough.

By the time he reached the warehouse, the woman was still unconscious, her breathing shallow but steady. He laid her on the table, adjusting her arms and legs until she was perfectly positioned, like a specimen in a lab. Thomas moved with methodical care, the way he had seen surgeons move when preparing a patient for surgery. There was a ritual to it—a kind of sacredness in the silence.

He removed the scalpel from the tray, the blade catching the dim light as he held it above her. His hand was steady. He didn't feel fear, only curiosity. What would it feel like? What would she look like beneath the skin, beneath the layers of flesh and muscle? He had always watched from a distance, but now he was the one making the incisions.

The first cut was slow, deliberate.

He dragged the blade lightly across her abdomen, watching as the skin parted with ease. Blood welled up around the incision, a bright, almost startling red against her pale skin. For a moment, Thomas froze, mesmerized by the sight. It was beautiful in a way he hadn't expected — organic, raw, and primal. He leaned closer, his breath shallow as he peeled back the layers of skin, exposing the tissue beneath.

His hand moved with confidence, making deeper incisions, exploring the body as if it were a puzzle to be solved. The organs beneath pulsed with life, even though she was unconscious, a silent reminder that she was still alive, at least for now.

But it wasn't enough. He needed to go deeper.

He continued his work, cutting slowly, methodically, watching her body respond to each new incision. The woman stirred slightly, her unconscious mind trying to fight against the drugs, but she was too far under. Thomas didn't stop. He didn't want to stop. Every cut was a revelation, a secret laid bare before him.

Hours passed before he was finally done. Her body, now a ruin of flesh and blood, lay still beneath him. Thomas stood back, breathing heavily, the scalpel still clutched in his hand. His heart pounded in his chest, the adrenaline still coursing through him. He looked down at his work and felt a strange sense of satisfaction, a feeling he hadn't known before.

He wiped the blade clean and set it back on the tray. The silence in the warehouse was deafening, the only sound his own ragged breathing. He knew he should be terrified, horrified by what he had done.

But instead, he felt... nothing. Or maybe it was everything. The power, the control—it was intoxicating.

For the first time in his life, Thomas felt truly alive.

Chapter 4: The Discarded

The warehouse was heavy with the metallic scent of blood. Thomas stood motionless, staring at the woman's mutilated body sprawled across the table, the lifeless form that had once been animated, full of fear and resistance. Now, she was nothing but flesh and bone—his creation, his work. He wiped his hands on the bloodstained apron and let the scalpel drop into a metal tray with a sharp clang.

For a moment, Thomas allowed himself to take in the aftermath. The deep red of her blood seemed almost vibrant against the stark, pale white of her exposed skin. The mess was monumental, larger than he'd anticipated. Her body was unrecognizable, carved open with surgical precision, yet still retaining an unsettling fragility.

It was beautiful in a grotesque way.

But reality tugged at the edges of his mind. The thrill had waned, replaced by a dull sense of urgency. What now? The euphoria that had coursed through him during the act had dulled, leaving the cold clarity of what needed to come next: disposal. He couldn't leave her here. This body—the evidence of his growing hunger—had to disappear completely.

Thomas glanced around the warehouse. It was an abandoned relic of industry, forgotten by the city, but even places like this weren't completely immune to discovery. He couldn't risk someone stumbling upon her remains.

He'd prepared for this. In theory, at least. But now that he stood before the grim aftermath of his own doing, the weight of it seemed heavier. She wasn't an animal carcass or a specimen to be incinerated in a lab; she was human. A person. And now she was his responsibility.

Thomas exhaled sharply, clearing his mind. No room for hesitation. He'd planned too carefully for this moment to be undone by sentiment. He approached the workbench where he kept his tools, taking out heavy-duty garbage bags and zip ties, along with the hacksaw he had stolen from the hospital's maintenance department weeks earlier. He rolled up his sleeves, knowing what came next wouldn't be as clean as the cuts he'd made before. This was manual labour, raw and brutal.

He approached the table, the saw's weight comfortable in his hands. The first cut into bone was harder than expected. The grinding sound filled the empty space, echoing off the walls of the warehouse. His arms ached as the saw gnawed through the flesh and bone, separating the limbs one by one. Arms first, then legs. He wiped the sweat from his forehead, ignoring the splatter of blood that had sprayed across his face.

The torso was the most difficult. The woman's body had been so delicate when he'd opened her up, the organs yielding easily to the scalpel. But now, the brutality of dismemberment made it all feel starkly different. He worked methodically, each cut precise, though his movements were growing heavier with fatigue. He placed the severed pieces into the garbage bags, one after the other, sealing them tightly.

By the time he finished, the air in the warehouse felt thick. His muscles burned, his hands sore from the constant pressure. He stepped back, looking at the six bags now sitting on the floor, filled with her remains. He had reduced her to nothing more than pieces. A jigsaw puzzle he would scatter and hide.

The next step required just as much thought. He couldn't simply dump the bags somewhere obvious. He had to ensure she was never found. That meant multiple locations — places where no one would think to look. Places that wouldn't raise suspicion.

Thomas had scouted these places in the weeks leading up to tonight. His knowledge of the city's underbelly had grown during his nocturnal wanderings. He knew the places where the desperate and the homeless gathered, where drug deals went unnoticed, and law enforcement rarely ventured. Abandoned lots, disused sewer entrances, even the river that wound its way through the outskirts of town.

He dragged the bags to his van, one by one, loading them into the back. The dark alley behind the warehouse provided cover, the rain masking the faint stench of blood that clung to him. His car was old, nondescript — perfect for blending in with the night.

As he drove, the city unfolded before him like a map. He navigated through empty streets, the rhythmic sound of rain against the windshield keeping him company. His thoughts were oddly clear, as if the enormity of what he'd done hadn't yet settled on his shoulders. His plan was simple: divide the body, leave no trace.

His first stop was a construction site on the edge of town. It was a place that had been dormant for months, left untouched by the developer's delays.

Thomas parked near a heap of debris and grabbed two of the bags. He slipped through a gap in the fence, careful not to disturb anything. The rain-soaked ground squelched beneath his boots as he made his way to a half-dug foundation. Without a sound, he tossed the first two bags into the mud-filled pit. They sank into the muck instantly, swallowed by the earth. He covered them with loose dirt, careful to leave no obvious signs of disturbance.

From there, he drove deeper into the countryside. His second stop was a quarry, long abandoned and now filled with stagnant water. Thomas hefted the remaining bags over his shoulder, one by one, and tossed them into the dark, still water. They vanished without a sound, ripples spreading across the surface and then fading into nothing. The quarry was deep, far too deep for anyone to recover the remains.

For the final piece — the torso — Thomas drove to the riverbank. The rain had swelled the river, making it faster, more violent. He pulled the last bag from the trunk, feeling its weight in his hands. It was the heaviest, the core of what she once was. He paused for a moment, staring at the rushing water. Then, with a grunt, he heaved the bag into the current. It was carried away instantly, swallowed by the darkness of the river, vanishing as if it had never existed.

Thomas stood on the riverbank, drenched in rain, his breath fogging in the cool night air. He had done it. The body was gone, scattered across the city and beyond. There would be no evidence left behind, no trace of the woman he had taken, dissected, and discarded.

The rain began to let up, a slow drizzle replacing the downpour. Thomas climbed back into his car, the adrenaline finally starting to ebb from his system. His hands were still shaking slightly as he gripped the steering wheel, but it wasn't from fear. It was from excitement. Satisfaction. He had pulled it off.

As he drove back to his apartment, his mind began to wander again. The next step wasn't disposal. The next step was the hunt. The ritual had been perfected, the method refined. But Thomas knew that this was only the beginning. There would be others, more bodies to dissect, more secrets to uncover.

The thought made him smile, a flicker of darkness behind his calm exterior. He was in control, for now. And with each body he discarded, with each life he took, he would only grow more powerful.

The city belonged to him now.

And somewhere, out there, his next victim was waiting.

Chapter 5: A New Hunger

The next day, Thomas returned to work as if nothing had happened. He moved through the hospital halls with the same quiet efficiency, greeting his coworkers with a nod and a polite smile. No one noticed the slight tremor in his hands, or the way his eyes lingered a little too long on the anaesthetic cart as he passed by.

It was all still there — the hospital, the operating theatres, the drugs. But now, they held a different meaning. They weren't just tools for healing anymore. They were a gateway, a means to something far more exhilarating.

As he went about his duties, his mind kept drifting back to the warehouse. The sensation of the scalpel in his hand, the feeling of power coursing through him, it was all-consuming. He had tasted something forbidden, something that now gnawed at him with a new hunger.

The hospital was full of opportunities.

The hospital's rhythm had always been predictable — controlled chaos wrapped in a veneer of professionalism. For years, Thomas had walked these halls, blending into the background, nothing more than a cog in the grand machinery of life-saving operations. But today, everything felt different. The constant beeping of monitors, the clatter of gurneys, and the murmurs of doctors had taken on a new texture — a dull hum compared to the vivid memory of last night.

He moved through his tasks with robotic precision, every action automated, but his mind was far away. Back in the warehouse, back with her. The cuts, the way her body yielded beneath the scalpel. The sight of her organs, the gleam of raw tissue. He could almost smell the sterile metal of the blade mingling with the coppery tang of blood. He wanted to feel it again.

But not yet. Patience. Control.

Thomas had always prided himself on his ability to stay disciplined. His life had been a carefully constructed routine — work, silence, anonymity. He couldn't let that unravel now. The investigation into the missing anaesthetic vials was ongoing, and though no one suspected him, one wrong move could ruin everything. He had to be careful.

For now, he would wait.

Later That Night

The clock struck midnight as Thomas stood in front of the mirror, studying his own reflection. He wondered what others saw when they looked at him. A quiet, unassuming man with plain features and tired eyes. Someone who blended in, invisible among the bustling doctors and nurses at the hospital. But under the surface, something was shifting.

In his small, dimly lit apartment, Thomas carefully prepared the tools he had collected over the years. Surgical knives, syringes, clamps, and other instruments that had been discarded or overlooked in the OR. He cleaned each one meticulously, relishing the feel of cold metal in his hands. They were an extension of him now, like a pianist's keys or a painter's brush. These instruments gave him control over life — over death.

He thought of the woman from last night, her face slack and peaceful as she slipped into unconsciousness. There had been a brief flash of fear in her eyes before the drugs had taken hold, a spark of life that he had snuffed out. But that had only been the beginning. There were more out there — countless others. The city was full of people who wouldn't be missed, people who wandered the streets at night without knowing they were being hunted.

And now, he craved the hunt. The control. The feeling of cutting into flesh, peeling back layers, watching as the body revealed its secrets.

But there was something more now, something new — a need for ritual. Last night had been impulsive, a test of his abilities. But this time, it would be different. It had to be. The next victim would be chosen carefully, the process executed with precision and care. There would be no mistakes.

Chapter 6: The Selection

Over the next few nights, Thomas became the predator. He scoured the city's streets, always late at night when the world was half-asleep. He observed the ebb and flow of people as they moved through the urban maze, their lives continuing as normal, blissfully unaware of the danger that stalked them.

He sat in a coffee shop on the outskirts of the city, the perfect vantage point. From there, he watched. He didn't know who he was looking for at first, only that he would know when he saw them. His eyes scanned the streets, searching for that one perfect person.

Then, he saw her.

She was sitting alone at a bus stop, fidgeting with her phone. Late twenties, maybe early thirties. Dark hair, a little worn out, perhaps coming home from a long shift. Something about her posture intrigued him — slumped, tired, defeated. There was a loneliness to her, an isolation that resonated with him. No one would miss her.

Thomas watched her from a distance, his pulse quickening. He observed her for days, following her subtly as she went about her routine. He memorized her schedule, learning when she left for work, when she returned, how she liked to take shortcuts through dimly lit alleyways. She lived alone. No family nearby. A ghost, just like him.

He prepared carefully. More of the anaesthetic had been smuggled from the hospital over the last week. He practiced the dosage again and again, making sure everything was perfect. He couldn't afford any mistakes this time. He had to savour the experience.

The Night of the Second Victim

It was raining when Thomas approached her. The streetlights flickered overhead, casting fractured shadows over the slick pavement. She was walking her usual route home, the hood of her coat pulled low over her head, unaware of the figure closing in behind her.

He had learned from his first kill. This time, his approach was smoother, more calculated. She didn't even hear him coming.

The moment his hand clamped down over her mouth, the soaked cloth already in place, she struggled. But Thomas was stronger than he appeared, his grip unrelenting. The chloroform mixture worked quickly, her thrashing growing weaker by the second. The fight left her body, and she slumped into his arms.

Thomas dragged her into a nearby alley, hidden from the street, and checked her pulse. Steady but faint. She was deeply unconscious, just as planned. He smiled to himself, the thrill building inside him once more.

The warehouse was ready, just as it had been before. He had improved the setup this time. More lighting, better tools, everything clean and in order. The table was laid out like a surgeon's operating table, the instruments gleaming in neat rows.

He laid her on the cold metal surface, arranging her body with the same care he had practiced at the hospital. Every detail mattered. This wasn't just about killing. It was an exploration. A ritual.

Thomas took his time, savouring every moment. He made the first incision with the same slow, deliberate precision as before, his breath steady, his heartbeat calm. He peeled back her skin, exposing the muscle underneath, the blood pooling softly on the table. The body was a work of art—intricate, complex, beautiful in its vulnerability.

Hours passed, just like before. But this time, Thomas felt more in control, more powerful. He had mastered the art of taking a life, of dissecting it piece by piece. It wasn't just curiosity anymore. It was something darker. Something deeper.

He wanted to feel her die beneath his hands. He needed to.

And when the final breath escaped her lips, he felt it—the rush of euphoria, the ultimate satisfaction of knowing he had taken everything from her. There was no guilt, no remorse. Only the cold, clinical understanding that he had become something more than human. He had become a force, a god in his own right.

When he finished, he stood back and admired his work, the light reflecting off the blood-soaked table. She was still, silent, lifeless. The perfect canvas.

He knew he would do it again.

Chapter 7: The Familiar Ritual

Thomas stood in the same warehouse, the sterile scent of bleach masking the lingering traces of blood from the first time. It was familiar now — almost comfortable. The scene before him was disturbingly similar to that night weeks ago: a body, lifeless, splayed on the table like an offering. This one had been easier, less resistance, less struggle. He had perfected the process.

He looked down at the woman's body, her limbs slack, her face forever frozen in a mixture of shock and fear. His hand hovered over her chest, feeling the faint warmth that still clung to her skin. He felt nothing for her, only the cold efficiency that had driven him the first time.

The hacksaw, still slightly dulled from the last use, sat on the table next to her, alongside the heavy-duty garbage bags and zip ties he'd brought again. He no longer trembled at the sight of the saw or hesitated before making the first cut. His mind was already moving ahead, planning each step with the precision of a craftsman. He had done this before. He could do it again.

And he would.

He rolled his shoulders back, easing the tension in his muscles before picking up the saw. The sound of metal grinding through bone filled the room, echoing off the steel walls of the warehouse. His arms moved mechanically, the saw tearing through flesh and ligaments with grim ease. There was no struggle to dismember her this time — his muscles had adjusted to the strain, the weight, and the horror of the task.

Each cut was cleaner, quicker than before. Arms, legs, torso—all neatly dismembered and placed into bags that he sealed tight. He felt none of the hesitation that had slowed him before. This time, his movements were swift, purposeful, and methodical, driven by the knowledge that he was perfecting his craft.

The body was reduced to parts within an hour, and the room fell silent. His breath came in slow, even waves, his heartbeat steady. The satisfaction was creeping in again—the same feeling of power that had washed over him after his first kill. This was what he was meant for. This was his purpose. Control.

He wiped the blood from his hands with a rag and moved to his van, once again pulling it around to the back of the warehouse. The heavy rain from the previous days had left the ground soft and muddy, but that didn't matter. The city was vast, and the places where he could hide his work were endless.

Just like last time, he loaded the bags into the trunk. The dark, lifeless night hung heavy as he drove through the empty streets. The streetlights flickered as he passed, casting faint shadows that clung to the corners of his vision. He gripped the wheel tightly, feeling the familiar twinge of anticipation rise in his chest. This was becoming routine, and he revelled in it.

He arrived at the same construction site where he'd buried the first body weeks before. The site had remained undisturbed, a sea of mud and unfinished concrete that stretched into the night. There were no lights, no workers, no one to see what he was about to do. He grabbed two of the bags and slipped through the same gap in the fence, his movements quicker, more confident this time. He didn't bother to look around nervously as he had the first time; he knew no one would come.

The pit from before had been filled slightly with rainwater, but that didn't deter him. He tossed the bags in, hearing the soft plop as they sank into the mud. The earth accepted them without a fight, swallowing the pieces like it had the first time. He covered them with loose dirt, smoothed over the surface, and stepped back. The rain had done its part to keep the ground soft, hiding any signs of disturbance.

His next stop was the quarry. It had become a place he knew intimately now, as if it had been waiting for him to come back. The stagnant water reflected the moonlight, casting a dull shimmer across its surface. He carried the remaining bags to the edge of the water, one by one, and dropped them in without a second thought. The water, dark and still, swallowed the bags whole, the surface barely rippling as it claimed its new secrets.

The final stop was the river. The routine was second nature now. The back of the van was lighter this time — only the torso remained. Thomas stood at the riverbank, the familiar rush of the water in his ears. The current was strong, pulling everything in its path downstream and away from the city. Without ceremony, he hefted the bag and hurled it into the water. It disappeared instantly, swept away by the violent surge of the river, the last piece of evidence gone.

Thomas watched the river for a moment longer, the sense of completion settling over him. There was no rush of adrenaline this time, no thrill. It was just... routine. He had gotten rid of her, just as he had the first.

As he turned to leave, his mind wandered once again to the future. He felt the familiar hunger creeping in, the itch of control that only grew stronger with each kill. The disposal process had been refined, perfected even. But the hunt? The hunt was what kept him coming back. It was always about the hunt.

His next victim was out there, somewhere. And Thomas knew it wouldn't be long before he would have to hunt again.

Back at the hospital, the tension was starting to build. More anaesthetic vials had gone missing, and this time, the staff was on edge. Thomas watched from the sidelines, careful to keep his face neutral, his expression blank as whispers began to circulate.

The police were involved now.

Chapter 8: The Investigation Tightens

The morning after his latest kill, Thomas stood at the nurses' station, pretending to review patient charts. The bright fluorescent lights buzzed above, and the air carried the sterile scent of disinfectant and latex. As usual, the hospital bustled with activity — nurses discussing rounds, doctors in hurried conversation — but today, there was something different in the air.

The missing anaesthetic was no longer a whisper among the staff. The investigation was intensifying, and the police had already begun questioning the theatre workers. Thomas knew it was only a matter of time before they reached him, but he remained calm, calculating his next move.

He overheard two nurses talking by the water cooler.

"I heard they're checking all the staff logs for the past month," one of them whispered, casting nervous glances around the room. "They think it's an inside job."

"Of course it's an inside job," the other nurse replied, her voice tense. "Who else would know how to access the vials without being seen?"

Thomas kept his eyes on the chart in front of him, his heartbeat steady. He knew better than to let the panic show. The vials he had taken had been staggered over weeks, small enough amounts to avoid immediate detection. Still, he couldn't afford to be careless now.

Later that day, as he prepared to leave, one of the hospital administrators approached him. "Thomas, could I have a word?"

He forced a polite smile and nodded. "Of course."

They led him into a small office, where two detectives sat waiting. One was a tall, broad-shouldered man with a clean-shaven face and sharp eyes. The other, a woman with dark hair tied in a tight bun, had an expression that gave away nothing.

"Thomas Greene, right?" the male detective said, flipping open a notebook. "We're investigating the recent theft of anaesthetic drugs from the hospital. We just need to ask you a few routine questions."

Thomas nodded, playing his part perfectly. "I've heard about the missing vials. What do you need to know?"

The questions started innocently enough—when had he last worked in the theatre, had he noticed anything unusual, were there any staff members acting suspiciously? Thomas answered them all with ease, keeping his responses brief and neutral.

But then the female detective leaned forward slightly, her eyes narrowing. "And where were you last night, Thomas? After your shift?"

There it was—the subtle shift. They were probing, testing his alibi. He felt the pressure building beneath his skin but didn't let it show.

"I was home," he answered smoothly, meeting her gaze. "I usually spend my evenings alone, reading or preparing for the next day's shift."

The male detective scribbled something down in his notebook, but his expression remained unreadable.

"Can anyone confirm that?" the woman pressed, her tone casual but firm.

Thomas shrugged. "I live alone. No one was with me, but I don't leave my apartment much after work. I value my quiet time."

The detectives exchanged glances, but they didn't push further. After a few more questions, they thanked him for his time and let him go.

As Thomas walked out of the office, his mind raced. They were getting closer, and the police were beginning to scrutinize the staff more intensely. He couldn't let his routine crack. He couldn't afford any missteps.

He left the hospital that day more alert than ever. His pulse pounded in his ears as he walked through the city, avoiding the familiar alleys he had once stalked. He knew now that he needed to be more cautious, more calculated with his next move. But the hunger was still there, gnawing at him, growing stronger with each passing day.

Chapter 9: The Third Victim

Days passed, and the pressure at work only mounted. The hospital tightened security around the anaesthetics, making it harder to access the drugs. Staff members were subjected to random searches, and the gossip grew louder with each missing vial. Thomas knew the window was closing, but the urge inside him was no longer something he could control.

He had already selected his next victim.

She was a nurse who worked late-night shifts in the emergency room, always staying well past midnight to help with overflow patients. Her name was Erica — early thirties, brown hair tied into a messy bun, and always with a tired smile for her patients. She was well-liked among the staff, her kindness genuine, her exhaustion apparent.

Thomas had watched her for weeks, memorizing her routine. She always left the hospital alone, taking the same dimly lit path toward the nearby train station. It was a quiet route, lined with closed shops and darkened windows. The perfect place for him to strike.

He planned meticulously, making sure everything would go smoothly. The anaesthetic dosage was prepared, the tools were ready, and the warehouse had been cleaned of any trace of his previous victims.

That night, he waited in the shadows just beyond the hospital, watching as Erica clocked out and walked toward the station. She moved slowly, her tired body weighed down by the day's work.

Thomas followed at a distance, his breath shallow, his heart beating faster as he neared her.

The streets were nearly empty, only the distant hum of cars in the background. He closed the gap between them, his fingers brushing the vial in his pocket. The moment was perfect.

Just as Erica passed a narrow alleyway, Thomas struck. He wrapped one arm around her neck, clamping the cloth over her mouth with the other. She struggled, but the fight was brief, her consciousness slipping away as the drugs took hold.

He dragged her limp body into the alley and then into the back of his van, which he had parked nearby in preparation. His pulse raced as he drove to the warehouse, his mind already thinking about the incisions, the slow dissection that awaited.

Once inside the warehouse, he laid Erica's unconscious body on the table, the tools gleaming beside her. He looked down at her, excitement and anticipation coursing through him. This was his third. And it would be perfect. Each time, the process felt more refined, more controlled. He knew what he was doing now — he was becoming better at it.

But as he picked up the scalpel, something unexpected happened.

Erica stirred.

His heart skipped a beat as her eyelids fluttered open, her eyes widening in confusion as she took in her surroundings. The anaesthetic dosage hadn't been enough. She was waking up.

Before Thomas could react, Erica let out a scream — loud, piercing, a sound that echoed off the concrete walls. Panic surged through him. He hadn't planned for this. His hands shook as he reached for the cloth again, desperate to silence her.

But Erica's scream had already shattered the silence of the night. Outside, in the darkness, a group of teenagers walking home from a nearby club stopped in their tracks. They exchanged confused glances before moving closer to the warehouse, curious about the noise.

Inside, Thomas struggled to control the situation, but it was already spiralling out of his grasp. Erica's scream had broken through the barrier of his carefully constructed world, and now, everything was falling apart.

For the first time, fear took hold of him.

The hunt was no longer thrilling. It was terrifying.

Chapter 10: Panic and Escape

Thomas's mind raced, every instinct telling him to flee, but he couldn't. He was frozen, trapped between the need to maintain control and the gnawing terror that everything was crumbling. Erica's scream had pierced through the carefully built walls of his fantasy. This wasn't how it was supposed to go.

Her eyes locked onto his, wide and filled with terror. She struggled weakly against her restraints, her movements sluggish from the remaining anaesthetic in her system, but she was awake — awake and aware.

Outside, Thomas heard voices. Footsteps. The teens who had heard the scream were getting closer, their laughter turning into hushed murmurs.

Panic surged through him. He had never been this close to getting caught before. His heart raced, the pounding in his ears growing louder with each passing second. This was no longer a controlled, clinical process — it was chaos.

Erica gasped for breath, her mouth opening to scream again, but Thomas was on her in an instant. He grabbed the cloth soaked with the remaining anaesthetic and shoved it over her face, pressing down with trembling hands.

"Quiet!" he hissed, his voice breaking, more to himself than to her.

Her body jerked, trying to fight, but the drugs finally took hold again, and she slumped, unconscious once more. He stood over her, his breath ragged, his hands shaking. The tools on the table gleamed under the single bulb, mocking him.

The voices outside grew louder, more distinct now.

"Did you hear that? It came from in here."

"Is someone messing around? Maybe it's squatters."

Thomas's heart sank. There was no way out of this. He could either finish the job quickly or run.

For the first time since his killing spree had begun, he felt powerless. The control he had prided himself on, the precise, methodical way he'd gone about his kills, had vanished. This wasn't art anymore. It was survival.

He glanced at Erica, lying on the table, her chest rising and falling slowly. She was still alive. Barely. His eyes darted to the tools beside her — the scalpel, the clamps, everything he had laid out for the slow, deliberate dissection he had planned. But now, none of it mattered.

Outside, the teenagers were growing bolder.

"Let's check it out. Could be someone in trouble."

Thomas's pulse quickened. He had to move now.

Without thinking, he grabbed the nearest tarp, hastily covering Erica's body. He couldn't kill her now — not with the possibility of being caught so close. He had to escape.

Moving swiftly, he gathered his tools, stuffing them into the bag he always carried. The evidence. He couldn't leave it behind. His hands fumbled as he zipped the bag shut, his mind racing for an escape plan.

The door to the warehouse rattled as one of the teens tried the handle. "It's locked. Should we break in?"

Thomas's blood ran cold. They were just outside. If they got inside, everything would be over.

He needed a way out. Fast.

In the corner of the warehouse, there was a side door — a small, rarely used exit that led to the alley behind the building. He had scouted the area weeks ago, planning every detail, and now it was his only hope.

Bag in hand, he sprinted across the warehouse, his footsteps echoing in the silence. He reached the door just as he heard the sound of breaking glass. The teenagers had found a way in.

With trembling fingers, Thomas unlocked the side door and slipped outside, his body pressed flat against the cold brick wall of the alley. He paused for a moment, listening to the voices inside the warehouse.

"Holy shit, look at this place! It's like some kind of horror movie!"

"Is that... is that blood?"

The panic inside him grew, but he couldn't afford to freeze now. Moving quickly, he ducked into the shadows of the alley, making his way down the narrow path that led back to the main street. His van was parked two blocks away. If he could make it there, he could disappear before anyone realized what had happened.

He kept his head down, his movements careful and calculated. The city streets were still mostly empty at this hour, the occasional passing car his only concern. He avoided the streetlights, keeping to the darkest parts of the road until he reached the van.

Throwing the bag into the passenger seat, he slid into the driver's side, his hands shaking as he gripped the steering wheel. He took a deep breath, trying to calm the storm raging inside him. He had gotten out. He had escaped.

But just barely.

He started the engine, the sound loud in the otherwise quiet night. His eyes flicked to the rearview mirror as he pulled away, scanning the street for any sign of the teens or the police. Nothing. He was in the clear, for now.

But the fear hadn't left him. He knew that this close call meant something had changed. His perfect system had failed. He had made a mistake.

And worse — Erica was still alive.

Chapter 11: The Fallout

Thomas didn't go back to the hospital the next day. He couldn't. Not with the chaos of the night still fresh in his mind. He stayed in his apartment, pacing the small living room as he replayed the events over and over.

Erica was alive. The teens had seen the inside of the warehouse. The police would be involved now. It was only a matter of time before everything came crashing down.

He checked the news obsessively, waiting for the inevitable report of a missing nurse or the discovery of the blood-soaked warehouse. But as the hours ticked by, there was nothing. No breaking news, no police investigation. Just the usual chatter about hospital shortages and minor crimes in the city.

Had the teens not called the police? Or had they not found Erica?

His mind raced with possibilities, each one worse than the last. He couldn't stay hidden forever. Sooner or later, he would have to go back to work, face his colleagues, and act as though nothing had happened.

The thought gnawed at him, the fear mixing with the same old hunger that never seemed to leave. It had been too close this time. But even now, he felt the pull of it again. The need for control, for that power over life and death.

But he couldn't risk it again. Not yet.

His phone buzzed on the counter, jolting him out of his thoughts. He picked it up and saw a text from one of his colleagues at the hospital.

"Hey, everything okay? We've had some weird stuff happen. Police were here asking about missing nurses."

Thomas's stomach dropped. So, it had begun.

His fingers hovered over the screen, struggling to come up with a response. He couldn't act suspicious. He had to stay calm, stay in control.

Finally, he typed back, "Yeah, I heard. I'm fine. Just taking a day off. What happened?"

The response came almost immediately.

"They said Erica's missing. Didn't show up for her shift today. No one can reach her. Everyone's freaking out."

Thomas's breath caught in his throat. Erica hadn't made it to the hospital. Which meant either she was dead, or she was somewhere else, still unconscious from the drugs. Either way, her disappearance was now being investigated.

His mind raced. He couldn't go back to the warehouse, not with the police involved. But he couldn't leave her alive either. If she woke up and told them what had happened, it would all be over.

He had to finish it

That night, as the city slept, Thomas made his way

Chapter 12: A Desperate Return

Thomas's knuckles whitened as he gripped the steering wheel, his breath shallow as he navigated the deserted streets. His mind was a whirlpool of panic and resolve, fear and focus. There was no way out now—he had to return to the warehouse. He had to finish what he started.

Every turn toward the industrial district felt like a step deeper into a labyrinth of his own making. The echoes of Erica's scream, the sight of her terrified eyes, haunted him. He had failed, and he wasn't used to failing. His methodical routine had been flawless until now, and that terrified him more than anything.

What if the police were already there? What if the teenagers had alerted them, and by now, they had found Erica's body? Would they be waiting for him?

His thoughts spiralled as the van crept closer to the warehouse, the dim glow of streetlights casting long shadows on the empty buildings. He parked a block away, hidden between two other vehicles. He couldn't afford to park close this time, in case anyone had returned to the scene.

Sliding out of the van, he moved quickly and quietly, sticking to the shadows. Every sound in the still night seemed amplified—the rustle of a plastic bag caught in the wind, the distant hum of traffic, the beating of his own heart in his ears.

The alley behind the warehouse was silent, just as he had left it. He scanned the surroundings, looking for any sign of life—any hint that someone had been here since his hasty escape. But there was nothing. The warehouse loomed dark and still, as if the horrors within had never happened.

His fingers trembled as he unlocked the side door, easing it open and stepping inside. The familiar, acrid smell of antiseptic and blood hit him immediately, mixed with the cold staleness of concrete. The dim light still flickered from the single bulb overhead, casting long shadows across the room.

The tarp still covered Erica's body on the table.

His pulse quickened. She was still there.

Moving cautiously, Thomas approached her. The tarp had shifted slightly, revealing part of her hand. He hesitated before pulling it back completely, revealing her pale face. Her breathing was shallow, her chest rising and falling faintly. She was alive — barely.

Relief washed over him, but it was quickly replaced by a renewed sense of urgency. She was still unconscious, still under the effects of the anaesthetic. But that wouldn't last much longer. He had to finish the job before she woke again.

This time, there would be no mistakes.

He pulled out the scalpel from his bag, his hands steadier now that he was back in his element. The chaos of the night faded into the background as he focused on the task before him. The fear subsided, replaced by the cold, calculated precision that had always guided him.

But just as he was about to make the first incision, there was a noise — a soft shuffle, almost imperceptible, coming from the far corner of the warehouse.

Thomas froze.

He hadn't heard anyone enter. He hadn't seen anything. But now, in the dim light, he realized something was wrong. His breath caught in his throat, and his hand instinctively tightened around the scalpel.

The noise came again, closer this time.

His eyes darted to the shadows, and then he saw it — a figure emerging from the darkness, moving slowly but deliberately toward him. His heart stopped.

It wasn't the police. It wasn't a random passerby.

It was one of the teenagers.

The boy, no older than sixteen, stood at the edge of the room, his face pale and his eyes wide with shock. He had followed the group here earlier, curious about the strange noises coming from the warehouse. But now, seeing the scene before him — the unconscious nurse, the blood, the scalpel in Thomas's hand — he was frozen in place, his body trembling with fear.

Thomas's mind raced. How long had the boy been there? Had he seen everything? Could he escape before the boy ran for help?

For a moment, their eyes locked — predator and prey, caught in a moment of suspended horror.

And then the boy bolted.

Without thinking, Thomas dropped the scalpel and ran after him. His legs propelled him forward, faster than he had ever moved, desperation and fear driving him. The boy was fast, his footsteps echoing through the empty warehouse as he sprinted toward the door. But Thomas was faster.

In seconds, he closed the distance between them, his hand reaching out and grabbing the boy's arm. The teen yelped in terror, struggling to break free, but Thomas's grip was like iron.

"Please—please, let me go!" the boy begged, his voice cracking.

Thomas didn't speak. He couldn't. His mind was too clouded, too consumed by the panic that had taken over. He dragged the boy back toward the darkened corner of the warehouse, away from the exit, away from the open streets where his screams could be heard.

"I won't tell anyone, I swear!" the boy cried, his voice frantic. "I didn't see anything!"

But Thomas knew that was a lie. The boy had seen too much.

There was no other choice now.

With one swift motion, Thomas pulled the boy to the ground, his hands closing around his throat. The boy kicked and struggled, his eyes wide with terror, but Thomas's grip only tightened. He couldn't afford to let him go—not now, not after everything.

The boy's struggling slowed, his limbs growing weak as the life drained from his body. Thomas's hands shook, but he didn't loosen his grip until the boy was completely still, his chest no longer rising, his eyes glassy and unfocused.

It was done.

Thomas sat back, gasping for breath, his mind reeling from the violence of it all. This wasn't how it was supposed to happen. This wasn't part of the plan.

He stood up, his body trembling, and looked down at the boy's lifeless form. His mind spun with a thousand thoughts, but none of them made sense. What had he done?

The killing of his victims had always been controlled — precise. But this… this was chaos. This was something else.

And now, there were two bodies in the warehouse.

Two loose ends.

Chapter 13: Cleaning Up

Thomas stared down at the boy's lifeless body, his mind a whirlwind of panic and disbelief. This wasn't supposed to happen. His plan had never involved killing a witness, let alone a child. But now, he had no choice. The boy had seen too much, and his presence here threatened everything. If the body was found, they would trace it back to him. There would be questions, investigations — things he couldn't control.

Thomas had no time to meticulously cut up the two bodies like before. The pressure was mounting, and he could feel the urgency weighing on him. With little choice, he hastily wrapped both bodies in thick, heavy tarpaulin, binding them tightly with rope. There would be no precision, no ritual tonight — just the need to make them disappear, fast.

The blood on his hands felt colder now, more sinister. He had killed before, but this was different. This was reckless.

The clock was ticking. He had to dispose of both bodies before the police came looking.

Erica was still unconscious, wrapped in the tarpaulin lying on the table, her chest rising and falling weakly. He couldn't leave her here, not with the boy's body beside her. He had to clean up everything — no evidence, no trail.

But as Thomas stood over her, he hesitated. The pull of curiosity, the fascination with his usual process, tugged at him again. The need to understand the human body, to explore its limits, surged through him. He wanted to continue his work — to finish what he had started with Erica.

But he couldn't , not this time

Not this time.

With gritted teeth, Thomas forced himself to move.

His usually steady, controlled nature was slipping through his fingers. He couldn't focus. Every nerve in his body was on edge, the calculated patience he once had now consumed by desperation. His breathing quickened as he glanced at the boy's lifeless form.

Two bodies. Two lives extinguished by his hand, and now he had to erase the evidence — dispose of them before anyone could find out what had happened.

The weight of his crimes pressed down on him, suffocating him, but he couldn't stop. There wasn't time. Every minute he spent here increased the likelihood of someone stumbling across the scene. The clock was ticking.

He grabbed the plastic sheet from the corner of the warehouse, the same one he'd used for cleanup before. Normally, he would have taken his time, ensuring every surface was spotless, but tonight was different. There was no time for his usual methodical process. The boy's body had complicated everything.

Thomas took a deep breath and surveyed the room. He would have to move fast — get both bodies out of the warehouse and into the van. He could drive them to the woods on the outskirts of town, where he had scouted an area weeks ago in case something went wrong. It was isolated enough to dispose of both bodies without attracting attention.

But as he bent down to lift Erica's unconscious form, a noise broke the silence.

The sound of footsteps. Heavy and deliberate, growing louder as they approached the warehouse door.

Thomas froze, his heart hammering in his chest. For a moment, he didn't breathe. Had the teenagers returned? Had they called the police?

The door rattled as the footsteps stopped just outside. Someone was there.

Panic surged through him. There was no time to hide the bodies, no time to escape. He glanced at the back door, considering a quick exit, but it was too late — the person outside would hear him leave.

The door creaked open.

Thomas's stomach twisted as a figure stepped into the dimly lit warehouse. The light from the single overhead bulb cast long shadows on the floor, distorting the man's features. It wasn't a teenager. It wasn't even the police.

It was a hospital security guard.

Thomas's pulse spiked as the guard stepped forward, his flashlight scanning the room. He hadn't noticed the bodies yet, but it was only a matter of time.

"Hello?" the guard called out, his voice steady, suspicious. "Someone in here?"

Thomas didn't answer. He couldn't. His brain was screaming for him to act, but he felt paralyzed. The guard moved closer, his flashlight beam sweeping across the floor.

And then it landed on the tarp-covered table. The body.

The guard froze, the realization dawning on him in an instant.

"What the—?" He stepped closer, pulling his radio from his belt. "I need backup at the warehouse on Wilcox Street. Possible—"

He didn't get the chance to finish.

In a blind panic, Thomas lunged at him, his body moving faster than his mind could process. He knocked the guard's radio from his hand, sending it skittering across the concrete floor. The guard stumbled backward, his eyes wide with shock as Thomas grabbed the scalpel from the table.

"No—wait!" the guard shouted, his hand going up in defence. "Please—"

But it was too late.

The blade flashed in the dim light as Thomas drove it into the guard's side, his hands shaking with the force of it. The guard gasped, his body buckling as he collapsed to the ground, blood seeping through his uniform. His eyes were wide, full of pain and disbelief, as he struggled to breathe.

Thomas stood over him, his chest heaving, the scalpel still clenched in his hand. The metallic scent of blood filled the air, sharp and overwhelming. The guard's body twitched, his breaths coming in shallow, ragged gasps, and then—silence.

For a long moment, Thomas just stood there, staring at the man he had just killed.

His third murder of the night. His fourth overall.

And now there was no turning back.

Chapter 14: Erasing Everything

The shock of killing the guard left Thomas disoriented, his mind a whirlwind of fear and disbelief. How had it come to this? His once-controlled, methodical approach had spiralled into something far more chaotic and violent. He had never intended for it to get this far — this messy.

But now, there was no other option. He had crossed a line, and there was no undoing it.

He had to erase everything.

The guard's radio still lay on the floor, its dull glow flickering as it emitted static. Backup could arrive at any moment. Thomas knew he had little time before someone came looking for the missing guard. He moved quickly, dragging the guard's body away from the door, his muscles straining as he hauled the heavy, lifeless form across the concrete.

The blood pooled beneath the body, leaving a stark red trail. Thomas's hands shook as he reached for more plastic sheeting, covering the area in a desperate attempt to hide the evidence. His mind raced, calculating his next move. He couldn't take all three bodies at once — there wasn't enough space in the van, and it would take too long.

He glanced at Erica's body, still unconscious on the table. She was supposed to have been his next experiment, but now she was just another problem. She had to disappear, just like the others.

But there was no time for precision. No time for his usual routine.

Thomas grabbed a pair of gloves from his bag and pulled them on, his breath coming in short, panicked gasps as he worked. He wrapped the guard's body in the remaining tarp, sealing it tightly. The boy's body was next, still small and limp, wrapped hastily in another sheet.

Finally, he turned to Erica. She was still alive, her body weak and unresponsive. He hesitated for a moment, his fingers hovering over her neck. He could end it now—finish her with a quick motion, a single cut to her throat. It would be simple.

But something stopped him.

He stared at her face, pale and unconscious, and for the first time, a flicker of doubt crept into his mind. This wasn't what he had wanted. Not like this. Not in the middle of this madness. He had been fascinated by the process, by the power of controlling life and death, but now… it all felt wrong.

With a growl of frustration, Thomas pulled back. There was no time for second-guessing. He wrapped Erica in another tarp and dragged her toward the back door of the warehouse. He'd have to load the bodies into the van one by one, taking care to avoid any passing cars or wandering eyes. It would take time, but it was the only way to erase the evidence.

The warehouse felt oppressive, the weight of his actions closing in on him as he worked. Every sound seemed louder—the scrape of the tarp, the clink of tools, the pounding of his own heart.

And then, as he was about to haul the guard's body toward the exit, his phone buzzed in his pocket.

For a moment, he froze, dread flooding his veins. Slowly, he pulled the phone out and glanced at the screen.

It was a message from his colleague at the hospital.

"Thomas, where are you? Police are at the hospital now, asking questions about Erica. They think she's been abducted."

Thomas's blood ran cold. The police were already involved. They were closing in on him, faster than he had expected.

He couldn't afford to be here when they found the warehouse. He couldn't afford any more mistakes.

His breath quickened as he looked down at the three bodies laid out before him. He had to move fast. If he could just get them to the woods, he could bury them — dispose of the evidence for good. There would be no more traces, no more loose ends.

But as he prepared to load the first body into the van, another thought crept into his mind.

What if it was too late? What if they were already watching him?

What if they were already on their way?

The panic surged through him again, but this time, it was different. This time, it wasn't just fear of being caught. It was fear of losing control — fear of the chaos he had unleashed, and the realization that he could never stop.

And for the first time since he had begun his dark, twisted journey, Thomas Greene felt something he hadn't expected.

Regret.

Chapter 15: The Closing Trap

The weight of the tarp seemed heavier than before as Thomas struggled to lift the guard's body into the van. His hands trembled, and his vision swam with panic-induced adrenaline. He couldn't think clearly anymore—every action felt rushed, sloppy. He was usually meticulous, but tonight, everything had gone wrong.

As he heaved the body into the back of the van, his mind spun with the possibilities. The police were asking questions at the hospital. His colleagues might be talking right now, their suspicions turning toward him. It wouldn't take long before someone mentioned his quiet, reclusive nature—someone who often worked alone, who knew the hospital layout better than most.

His hands gripped the edges of the van door, the cool metal grounding him for a brief moment. He had to act fast, think clearly. If he could dispose of the bodies, cover his tracks, he might still be able to escape. But deep down, a voice nagged at him, whispering that it was already too late.

The rain began to fall as he returned to the warehouse for the boy's body. Each raindrop sounded like a gunshot in the empty alleyway. He hurried, sweat beading on his forehead despite the cool night air. The tarp slid against the wet concrete as he dragged the second body toward the van.

In the distance, he heard sirens.

His heart stopped.

They were coming.

Without hesitation, Thomas threw the boy's body into the back of the van and slammed the doors shut. The third body — Erica — still lay inside the warehouse, but there wasn't enough time to go back for her now. The sirens were getting closer, their wailing growing louder by the second.

He couldn't leave Erica behind. If the police found her alive, she would talk. She would tell them everything. But there was no time to dispose of her properly. He would have to return later — if he had the chance.

Thomas ran around to the driver's side of the van, his fingers fumbling as he tried to unlock the door. His pulse thundered in his ears, his breath coming in shallow gasps. Finally, he yanked the door open and jumped into the driver's seat, slamming the door behind him.

The sirens were close now. Too close.

With trembling hands, he started the engine and pulled out of the alley, his knuckles white on the steering wheel. He forced himself to stay calm, to drive slowly and carefully, even though every instinct screamed at him to floor the gas and get as far away as possible.

The rain fell harder, splattering against the windshield, obscuring his view of the road ahead. He turned the wipers on, their rhythmic swishing doing little to calm his nerves. Every flash of headlights made him flinch, every intersection felt like a trap waiting to spring.

As he drove, his mind raced. Where could he go? The woods were still an option, but they were too far away. He couldn't risk driving out of the city with the bodies in the back, not with the police likely setting up roadblocks soon. He needed somewhere closer — somewhere he could hide, at least for a few hours.

His thoughts were interrupted by the sudden flash of blue lights in his rearview mirror.

A police car.

His stomach twisted into a knot as the patrol car pulled up behind him. The lights weren't flashing, and the siren was off, but the vehicle stayed close, matching his speed. He forced himself to breathe, to stay calm. The cop didn't know what he was carrying. They hadn't stopped him. Maybe they were just patrolling the area.

Or maybe they were waiting for him to make a mistake.

The police car followed him for several agonizing minutes, every second stretching into an eternity. Thomas gripped the wheel tighter, sweat dripping down his forehead. He kept his speed steady, obeying every traffic law, trying to appear as normal as possible. He glanced at the clock on the dashboard, watching the seconds tick by.

Then, just as suddenly as they had appeared, the police car turned off onto another street, disappearing into the rain.

Thomas exhaled, his muscles going slack with relief. He hadn't realized he'd been holding his breath. His hands were slick with sweat, his fingers numb from gripping the steering wheel so tightly.

But he couldn't relax. Not yet. Not until he was far away from the city, far away from everything he had done.

Chapter 16: Desperate Decisions

Thomas drove aimlessly for the next hour, his mind racing with half-formed plans and fading confidence. The rain continued to pound the streets, and the late hour ensured that the roads were almost deserted. Every time he passed a parked police car or heard distant sirens, his heart leapt into his throat.

He couldn't keep driving with the bodies in the back. He needed to get rid of them — now.

Finally, he turned off the main road and followed a narrow, winding path that led to an abandoned construction site on the outskirts of the city. It was a place he had scouted weeks earlier, just in case things went wrong. Tonight, it would have to serve as his burial ground.

The rain made the dirt roads slippery, and the van's tires skidded as he pulled up to the site. There was no one around — no workers, no security. The half-finished skeletons of buildings loomed in the darkness, their exposed beams dripping with rain.

Thomas parked the van behind one of the large concrete structures, far enough from the main road to avoid being seen. He killed the engine and sat in silence for a moment, gathering his thoughts. The bodies in the back felt like an anchor pulling him deeper into the abyss.

This was it. He had to get rid of them. Now or never.

He opened the back doors of the van, the smell of death hitting him full force. The bodies lay there, wrapped in their tarps, lifeless and cold. The guard's body was heavier than the others, his limbs stiff with rigor mortis. The boy's body was small and pitiful, a stark reminder of the chaos Thomas had created.

With the rain pouring down, Thomas worked quickly, dragging the bodies one by one to the edge of the construction site. He had brought a shovel, but the ground was too wet and muddy to dig a proper grave. Instead, he pulled the bodies into one of the large, unfinished drainage ditches that lined the site. The deep pit would have to suffice until he could return to deal with the bodies properly.

As he dropped the guard's body into the ditch, the tarp caught on a piece of rebar, ripping open and exposing the man's face. His eyes stared blankly up at the rain, and for the first time, Thomas felt a wave of nausea roll through him. He had killed a man—a man who had done nothing but his job. A man who had stumbled into Thomas's nightmare by accident.

Thomas turned away, his stomach churning. He couldn't think about that now. He had to finish this.

The boy's body came next, smaller and lighter. Thomas forced himself not to look at the child's face as he heaved him into the pit, the tarp sinking into the mud. The rain had turned the ground into a swamp, and the bodies were quickly covered in a layer of muck and debris. It wasn't perfect. It wasn't clean. But it would have to do.

Thomas wiped the rain from his face, his entire body trembling with exhaustion. The rain had soaked him to the bone, and the cold air bit at his skin. He had done what he could to hide the bodies, but he knew they wouldn't stay hidden forever.

He had to go back for Erica.

Chapter 17: The Return

The rain had let up slightly by the time Thomas drove back to the warehouse. His mind was frayed, his nerves shot. He had gotten rid of two bodies, but the third was still waiting for him. Erica was still alive — still a threat. He couldn't leave her here, not with the police closing in.

As he pulled up to the warehouse, the hair on the back of his neck stood on end. Something wasn't right. The alley was quiet, the streets empty, but there was a tension in the air — a heaviness that hadn't been there before.

He parked the van and approached the warehouse, his eyes scanning the shadows for any sign of movement. The door was still slightly ajar, just as he had left it.

Thomas stepped inside, his heart pounding in his chest.

And then he saw it.

Erica was gone.

The tarp lay crumpled on the floor, stained with blood, but her body was missing.

For a moment, Thomas couldn't process what he was seeing. He had left her unconscious - helpless. There was no way she could have escaped. And yet, the table was empty. The restraints were gone.

Panic gripped him as his mind raced through the possibilities. Had she woken up and fled? Had someone found her and taken her away? Had the police arrived while he was disposing of the other bodies?

His eyes darted around the warehouse, searching for any clue, any sign of where she might have gone. But there was nothing.

Then, from somewhere in the distance, he heard a noise.

A faint sound — a shuffle of footsteps, followed by the creak of a door opening.

Thomas's blood ran cold.

Someone was here.

Chapter 18: The Hunter Becomes Hunted

The faint sound of footsteps echoed through the warehouse, bouncing off the cold concrete walls. Thomas's heart pounded in his chest as he froze, his ears straining to pick up the direction of the noise. It was coming from somewhere deeper inside the building, toward the back — toward the exit.

Someone was still here. And it wasn't Erica.

The panic that had been gnawing at him since the moment he discovered her body missing flared into full-blown terror. His mind raced, scrambling to make sense of the situation. Had she escaped? Was she being helped? Or worse — was this a trap?

His hands, still slick from the rain and mud, reached into his jacket pocket, clutching the scalpel he always carried with him. The cold steel gave him a momentary sense of control, though he knew that feeling was fleeting. The warehouse had turned from a place of his dark experiments into a hunting ground — only this time, it wasn't he who was hunting.

The creaking of a door ahead of him snapped him back to the present. The sound was clearer now, closer. Whoever it was hadn't left yet.

Thomas edged toward the back of the warehouse, his footsteps silent on the slick floor. The rain outside had slowed to a drizzle, but the heavy air inside felt thick, oppressive, like a vice closing around him. He couldn't let himself get cornered.

He moved carefully, his pulse quickening with each step. His eyes adjusted to the dim light, scanning every shadow, every corner for movement. If Erica had managed to escape and somehow found help, it would all be over. Everything. His entire life as he knew it would collapse in a single night. He could almost feel the jaws of the trap closing around him.

Then, a flicker of movement caught his eye.

Near the far exit, in the darkest part of the warehouse, a figure stood still, barely visible. It was too far to make out any details, but someone was there — someone watching.

His breath caught in his throat as he gripped the scalpel tighter. He couldn't wait any longer.

Without thinking, Thomas surged forward, the cold fear turning into raw adrenaline. He had to stop this — he had to regain control. The figure ahead shifted, as if startled by his sudden approach, and began moving quickly toward the exit.

But Thomas was faster.

His legs carried him across the slick concrete floor in a few long strides, his heart hammering as the figure neared the door. He couldn't let them get away — not without knowing what they had seen, what they knew.

Just as the figure reached for the handle, Thomas lunged, grabbing them by the shoulder and spinning them around. His scalpel flashed in the faint light, the cold metal gleaming in his hand.

"Who are you?" he snarled, his voice tight with panic. "Where's Erica?"

The figure recoiled, and as the dim light caught their face, Thomas's heart sank.

It wasn't Erica.

It was the boy — the same boy from earlier. The one he had killed.

Or had he?

Thomas's mind reeled as he stared at the boy's pale, wide-eyed face. It didn't make sense. He had watched the boy die — he had felt the life drain from his body as he strangled him. How was he standing here now, alive?

The boy's mouth opened, but no sound came out. His eyes were wide with fear, locked on the scalpel in Thomas's hand. Blood still stained his clothes from earlier, but there was no sign of injury, no wound where the boy should have died.

Thomas felt the world spin around him. This wasn't real. It couldn't be. The boy was dead. He had killed him. Hadn't he?

The boy finally spoke, his voice barely a whisper. "You... you can't stop this."

Thomas's grip tightened on the scalpel, his knuckles white. His breath came in short, shallow gasps, his mind screaming at him to do something, anything to regain control of the situation. But the boy's words hung in the air, suffocating him.

"You can't stop this."

Before Thomas could respond, the door behind the boy swung open with a loud creak. Bright light flooded the dark warehouse, blinding him for a moment. He stumbled back, instinctively raising his arm to shield his eyes.

When his vision cleared, he saw them.

Two figures, standing in the doorway, silhouetted against the rain. And in front of them, Erica.

She was standing—alive, conscious—her eyes wide with terror. Her clothes were torn, her face pale, but she was standing on her own two feet. Somehow, she had escaped. Somehow, she had survived.

And she wasn't alone.

Behind her stood two police officers, their hands on their weapons, their eyes locked on Thomas.

"Drop the weapon!" one of them shouted, his voice cutting through the air like a blade. "Now!"

Thomas's heart plummeted. The realization hit him like a freight train. This was the end. There was no escaping this. Everything he had done—everything he had tried to hide—was about to come crashing down around him.

His mind raced. He couldn't go to prison. He couldn't be exposed, stripped of the power he had held over life and death. This wasn't how it was supposed to end.

Erica's eyes met his across the warehouse, her expression a mixture of fear and confusion. She had seen everything. She knew what he had done. And now, with the police standing behind her, she had won.

Thomas's hand trembled as he stared down at the scalpel in his grip. For the first time in his life, he felt truly powerless.

"Drop the weapon!" the officer shouted again, his voice louder, more forceful.

Thomas's mind reeled, his thoughts scattering in every direction. There was no escape. No more control. No more carefully constructed plans. Only chaos and the suffocating weight of his crimes.

The boy's voice echoed in his mind again.

"You can't stop this."

Thomas let out a breath, his fingers loosening around the scalpel. It clattered to the floor, the sharp sound echoing in the cavernous warehouse.

The officers rushed forward, their guns drawn, but Thomas didn't resist. His body felt numb, his thoughts distant, as they forced him to the ground, his hands wrenched behind his back. Cold metal cuffs bit into his wrists, but he didn't feel the pain. All he could think about was how it had all spiralled out of control.

As they dragged him to his feet and led him toward the door, Thomas's eyes flicked to Erica one last time. She stood frozen, her eyes still locked on his, but now there was something else in her gaze — something he couldn't quite place.

And then, as the officers pushed him out into the rain, into the blinding light, Thomas realized what it was.

Pity.

Chapter 19: The Aftermath

The trial was swift, the evidence overwhelming. Erica's testimony, the boy's escape, the blood in the warehouse — all of it painted a clear picture of a monster, a man who had killed without remorse, who had used his position in the hospital to prey on the vulnerable.

Thomas sat silently throughout the proceedings, his face expressionless, as the prosecution laid out the grisly details of his crimes. The bodies found at the construction site, the missing drugs from the hospital, the failed attempt to silence Erica — it was all too much to deny.

The media had a field day, branding him "The Theatre Killer," a man who had taken the tools of healing and turned them into instruments of death. His quiet, unassuming nature only added to the horror — the idea that someone so ordinary could harbour such dark desires.

But through it all, Thomas felt nothing. The power, the control he had once craved, was gone. He was no longer the one in control of life and death. He was just a prisoner now, waiting for the inevitable.

As the judge read out the guilty verdict, sentencing him to life without the possibility of parole, Thomas barely flinched. He had known this was coming from the moment they had found him in the warehouse. There had been no escape.

But as he was led away in shackles, the image of Erica's face lingered in his mind. The pity in her eyes. The knowledge that she had survived, that she had outlasted him.

In the end, it was she who had won.

Or had she !
- [ ]

Chapter 20: Life Behind Bars

The metal door of the prison cell clanged shut behind Thomas with a heavy finality. The sound reverberated through the concrete walls, echoing in his mind like the closing of a coffin. This was his life now — four walls, a thin cot, and the ever-present hum of prison life around him. Guards patrolled the corridors, their heavy boots scuffing the floor. Inmates shouted to one another, their voices filled with boredom and hostility.

Thomas sat on the edge of his cot, staring at the floor, his mind a haze of thoughts that led nowhere. The trial had been swift, the evidence insurmountable. They hadn't even needed to delve into the more gruesome details of his crimes to secure the conviction. There was no point in arguing, no point in defending himself. He had been caught, exposed for what he was, and now he was serving the consequences.

Life without the possibility of parole.

He had replayed the events that led him here a thousand times, but the conclusion was always the same. He had been meticulous, careful, precise in every step of his twisted rituals. Yet, the hunger for control, for that power over life and death, had led him to lose the very thing he craved the most — control. In the end, chaos had swallowed him whole.

The prison air was thick with the stench of sweat, rust, and something else that was harder to place — desperation, perhaps. He had heard rumours that other inmates knew who he was. "The Theatre Killer." The media had painted him as a monster, and in here, monsters were treated with a special kind of disdain. Even among the hardened criminals, Thomas knew he was different.

The door to his cell slid open, breaking him from his thoughts. A guard stood at the entrance, his face impassive.

"Visitor," he grunted, stepping aside to let Thomas pass.

A visitor? Thomas hadn't expected anyone to come. No family, no friends — he had kept his life so insulated that no one should care enough to see him now. Curious, and with no other choice, Thomas followed the guard down the narrow corridor, his mind racing through possibilities. Was it Erica? Had she come to confront him one last time? Or was it the police, coming to extract one final confession?

The visiting room was bleak and sterile, a place where hope rarely lived. A long row of booths separated the prisoners from the visitors, each with a glass divider and a phone to speak through. Thomas sat down in the designated booth, his eyes scanning the other side.

Then he saw the visitor.

It wasn't Erica.

It was the boy.

The same boy he had killed — or thought he had killed. The boy he had seen alive again in the warehouse, standing there, as real as the day he had choked the life out of him.

Thomas blinked, his body going cold. This couldn't be real. This wasn't possible.

The boy sat down in the chair opposite him, his face calm, though his eyes held a knowing glint that sent a chill through Thomas's bones. The boy picked up the phone on his side of the glass, gesturing for Thomas to do the same.

Thomas hesitated, his hand hovering over the receiver. He couldn't understand how this was happening. How was the boy here? He had seen him die. He had felt his body go limp beneath his hands. But now, here he was, sitting before him in this cold, sterile room.

Slowly, as if in a daze, Thomas picked up the phone, holding it to his ear.

The boy's voice was soft, but it carried a weight that made Thomas's skin crawl.

"You thought it was over," the boy said, his eyes locked onto Thomas's. "But it's not."

Thomas's grip tightened on the phone, his mind struggling to comprehend what he was hearing. The boy's voice was calm, far too calm for someone who had been a victim. There was no fear in his eyes, no anger. Only a strange, unsettling certainty.

"You think prison walls can keep you safe from what you've done?" the boy continued, leaning closer to the glass. "You think you can hide from your guilt in here, pretend it's all behind you?"

Thomas swallowed hard, his throat dry. This couldn't be happening. He was losing his mind.

"I don't understand," Thomas muttered, his voice weak. "You're... you're dead."

The boy smiled, a cold, unsettling smile that made Thomas's stomach turn.

"Dead?" the boy repeated, almost amused. "Do you really believe death is the end of this? You may have taken my life, but you've unleashed something much worse."

Thomas felt a wave of nausea rise in his chest. He had been meticulous, careful with every detail. The boy's death had been clean—clinical. He had controlled it. But this... this was beyond anything he could comprehend.

The boy leaned back in his chair, his eyes never leaving Thomas's.

"You've crossed a line, Thomas," the boy said softly. "And now, there's no going back. You'll never escape what you've done."

Thomas felt the phone slipping from his hand, his body numb with fear. This couldn't be real. It was a hallucination, a manifestation of his guilt. His mind was playing tricks on him, punishing him for his crimes in ways he had never anticipated.

But the boy didn't disappear.

He just sat there, staring at Thomas, his gaze steady and unblinking.

Then, without another word, the boy stood up and walked away, leaving Thomas alone in the visiting room, his mind spiralling into a void of confusion and terror.

The guard returned moments later, his face as indifferent as before.

"Time's up," the guard said, motioning for Thomas to stand.

Thomas didn't move. He couldn't. His legs felt like lead, his body heavy with the weight of what he had just seen. Or thought he had seen.

The boy had been dead. He was certain of it.

Wasn't he?

Chapter 21: The Long Descent

The days in prison bled together, each one more suffocating than the last. Time had lost all meaning for Thomas. He barely ate, barely slept. His mind was a constant fog, haunted by visions of the boy — visions he couldn't explain, couldn't escape.

At night, in the darkness of his cell, the boy's face would appear in the shadows, his voice echoing in Thomas's ears.

"You thought it was over. But it's not."

He had tried to convince himself that it wasn't real — that it was a hallucination, a side effect of the guilt that had been gnawing at him since the day he was caught. But no matter how hard he tried to shake the feeling, the boy's presence lingered, always just out of reach, always waiting in the corners of his mind.

The other prisoners gave him a wide berth. They had heard the stories, knew what he had done. They called him a freak, a monster. They didn't know the half of it.

And then, one night, the boy came to him again.

Thomas lay in his cot, staring up at the ceiling, his body stiff with exhaustion. The guards had just completed their nightly rounds, and the prison was quiet, save for the occasional cough or murmur from the other cells.

But then, from the darkness, came a soft whisper.

"You can't hide from me."

Thomas bolted upright, his heart pounding in his chest. The cell was empty, as it always was, but the boy's voice lingered, curling around him like a noose tightening with each word.

"You can't escape this, Thomas. You'll never escape."

Thomas clutched his head, his fingers digging into his scalp as he tried to block out the voice, but it only grew louder, more insistent.

"I'm with you now. Always."

It was too much. The guilt, the fear, the madness. It had all caught up to him, and now it was dragging him down into an abyss from which he would never return.

And as the darkness closed in, Thomas realized with a sickening certainty that the boy had been right all along.

He couldn't stop this.

There was no escape.

Chapter 22: The End of the Line

The final weeks of Thomas's life were spent in a haze of madness and fear. The boy's voice never left him, always whispering, always taunting, driving him deeper into insanity. No one else heard it, no one else saw the boy—but Thomas did. He saw him in every shadow, every reflection, every flicker of light that danced across the cold prison walls.

In the end, it wasn't the justice system that punished him.

It was his own mind.

When the guards found him one morning, his body limp and lifeless on the floor of his cell, they didn't know what had happened. There were no signs of struggle, no wounds. It was as if he had simply given up, as if his mind had finally broken under the weight of his own guilt.

But in the corner of the cell, in the dim light of the early morning, there was something else— something that only Thomas could see.

The boy.

Standing there, watching.

And smiling.

The story of Thomas Greene—the "Theatre Killer"—faded into the annals of prison folklore, a tale of a man consumed by his own darkness. Some said he had gone mad with guilt, others believed his crimes had finally caught up with him. But those who had known him, those who had worked alongside him at the hospital, whispered of something else.

Something darker.

And in the quiet corners of the prison, where the shadows ran deep and the whispers of long-dead men clung to the walls, there was something darker still. The story of Thomas Greene, "The Theatre Killer," became a chilling tale passed among inmates and guards alike—yet no one could explain what had truly broken him in those final days.

Some said his crimes had rotted his mind. Others believed in something more sinister, something unnatural. Rumours spread like wildfire, each more twisted than the last. People spoke of how prisoners on the night shift claimed to hear faint whispers near Thomas's old cell, whispers that weren't just the wind. They said it was the voice of a boy, calling out in the darkness, taunting whoever dared to listen.

In the months following Thomas's death, strange things began to happen. Guards patrolling Cell Block D—the area where Thomas had been housed—often reported a feeling of being watched, as if unseen eyes followed them in the dim light. Some even swore they saw fleeting glimpses of a young boy standing just at the edge of their vision, vanishing the moment they turned their heads.

One guard, a veteran of the prison for over two decades, refused to work the night shift anymore. His story was the same as many others, but his fear was palpable when he described the last night he had patrolled Cell Block D. He'd heard a voice, soft and clear, just like the others. But this time, it spoke his name.

A voice that didn't belong to any of the prisoners.

It called out, "You can't stop this."

A Year Later

The hospital where Thomas once worked carried on as usual. Patients came and went, surgeries proceeded like clockwork, and new staff replaced the old. The investigation into the missing anaesthetics had been resolved, and the murders that once shocked the city faded into the background as newer crimes took over the headlines.

But the operating theatres — the very places where Thomas had spent his time — began to develop their own strange stories.

It started with little things. A missing tool, always the same scalpel, found later in places it shouldn't have been. Lights flickering during operations, casting strange shadows on the walls. Nurses complained of cold drafts that seemed to come from nowhere, even in fully sealed rooms.

Then, there were the incidents with the patients.

In three separate cases, patients under anaesthesia reported seeing a young boy standing at the edge of the operating table. They described him with startling consistency — a pale face, wide eyes, and a slight, sad smile. None of the medical staff could explain it, and no one had seen anything unusual during the surgeries.

But the patients insisted.
The boy was always there, watching.

Chapter 23: Something watching

Erica, the sole survivor of Thomas Greene's madness, had tried to move on with her life. After testifying at the trial, she had distanced herself from everything related to the case, transferring to a different hospital and seeking counselling to cope with the trauma.

But the nightmares never stopped.

In her dreams, she was back in the warehouse, strapped to the table, Thomas standing over her with the scalpel. The cold steel glinted in the faint light, and she could feel the weight of his gaze as he prepared to cut into her skin. But just before the blade touched her, another figure always appeared — watching from the shadows.

The boy.

Each time, he stood just out of reach, his wide eyes filled with something Erica couldn't quite place — sadness, pity, or perhaps something darker. He never spoke, but his presence was overwhelming, filling the air with a suffocating sense of dread.

No matter how much therapy she attended or how hard she tried to bury those memories, the boy haunted her dreams, just as he had haunted Thomas in the end.

One night, after months of nightmares, Erica woke suddenly, drenched in sweat. She glanced around her bedroom, heart pounding, half expecting to see the boy standing at the foot of her bed. But the room was empty, the darkness undisturbed.

She took a deep breath, trying to calm herself, but a strange feeling settled over her — a sense of being watched. She told herself it was nothing, just the remnants of her nightmare. She reached for the glass of water on her bedside table, her hand shaking slightly.

But as she raised the glass to her lips, she saw it.

A faint reflection in the glass.

The boy.

Standing in the corner of the room, his eyes locked onto hers, his expression unchanged.

Erica gasped, dropping the glass, which shattered on the floor. She scrambled out of bed, her pulse racing, but when she looked again, the boy was gone. The room was empty once more, but the feeling of his presence lingered in the air like a heavy fog.

She backed away slowly, her breath coming in short, panicked bursts, her mind racing to make sense of what she had just seen. But deep down, she knew.

It wasn't over.

Whatever had happened to Thomas, whatever darkness he had unleashed, it hadn't died with him.

It had followed her.

And just like Thomas, she realized with chilling clarity, there was no escape.

The Shadow Lingers

The story of Thomas Greene, the "Theatre Killer," became the stuff of urban legends, whispered among medical staff and prison guards alike. But those who had been close to the case—those who had felt the shadow that followed him—knew there was something more. Something that couldn't be explained by guilt or madness.

Something darker.

The boy remained.

In the shadows of the operating theatres, in the cold corners of the prison, and in the minds of those who had crossed paths with Thomas, the boy lingered. Silent, watchful, waiting.

And those who had seen him knew the truth.

You couldn't escape him.

Not now.

Not ever.

Chapter 24: Unseen Eyes

Erica couldn't shake the feeling that she wasn't alone. Ever since that night—the night she had seen the boy's reflection in the glass—her life had spiralled into something unfamiliar and unsettling. No matter where she went, no matter how many times she reminded herself it wasn't real, she felt his presence.

At work, in the grocery store, in the silence of her apartment—he was there, just out of sight, like a shadow she couldn't outrun. She'd wake up drenched in sweat, the image of his wide, unblinking eyes seared into her mind. It had gotten so bad that she stopped sleeping for more than an hour or two at a time, afraid that she would see him again in her dreams.

She had stopped talking to people about it, too. Her therapist had dismissed it as a trauma response, a manifestation of survivor's guilt, but that didn't explain what she had seen. What she knew she had seen.

The boy was real.

He wasn't just a ghost haunting her mind. He had been there, at the foot of her bed. She had seen him with her own eyes.

And now, he wouldn't leave her alone.

The hospital was the only place where Erica felt some semblance of normalcy. The routine of work, the constant movement, the steady hum of machines—it all distracted her, kept her grounded in the present. But even the hospital, a place she had once found comfort in, was changing.

The operating theatres felt different now. Colder, darker, more oppressive. Nurses whispered about strange occurrences — the flickering lights, the missing tools, the feeling of being watched. Some claimed it was just stress, or exhaustion from the long hours. But Erica knew better.

She had heard the rumours about the patients who had seen the boy during surgery. They described him just as she had seen him — pale, with wide, sad eyes. He never spoke, but his presence was impossible to ignore. Erica had tried to convince herself it was just coincidence, but the more she heard, the more she realized the truth.

He wasn't just haunting her.

He was haunting the hospital.

One evening, while preparing for a late surgery, Erica caught a glimpse of something out of the corner of her eye. She was standing in Operating Theatre 3, organizing the sterile instruments when she saw movement near the door. It was just a flicker, a shadow darting across the floor, but it was enough to make her freeze.

Her heart raced as she turned to face the door, but there was nothing there. Just the cold, empty hallway.

She exhaled slowly, trying to calm her racing pulse. Maybe it was just her nerves. She hadn't slept well in days, and the exhaustion was starting to take its toll. She shook her head, trying to shake off the paranoia.

But as she turned back to the instrument tray, she felt it again.

That sense of being watched.

Her skin prickled, the hairs on the back of her neck standing on end. She glanced around the room, her eyes scanning every corner, every shadow, but she saw nothing. The operating theatre was empty, save for the hum of the fluorescent lights overhead.

Then, from behind her, came a soft, almost imperceptible sound — a faint shuffle of footsteps.

Erica's breath caught in her throat. Slowly, she turned around, her heart pounding in her chest.

And there he was.

The boy.

Standing in the doorway, his pale face illuminated by the harsh overhead light. His wide, sad eyes locked onto hers, and for a moment, the world seemed to stop.

Erica couldn't move. She couldn't speak. She could only stare, frozen in place, as the boy took a step closer. His bare feet made no sound as they touched the cold tile floor, but his presence filled the room, suffocating her with an overwhelming sense of dread.

He took another step, his eyes never leaving hers.

And then he whispered, in a voice so soft it was barely audible:

"You can't stop this."

Erica's breath came in short, panicked gasps. Her hands shook as she backed away, her eyes wide with terror. The boy took another step forward, his small, fragile frame almost ghostlike in the sterile light of the operating theatre.

"You can't escape," he whispered again, his voice carrying an eerie calmness that chilled her to the bone.

Erica stumbled backward, her back hitting the cold metal counter behind her. Her mind screamed at her to move, to run, to get away, but her body refused to obey. She was trapped — pinned in place by the boy's unblinking gaze.

And then, just as quickly as he had appeared, the boy was gone.

Erica blinked, her vision swimming as she tried to make sense of what had just happened. The doorway was empty, the room silent except for the steady hum of the lights.

Her legs gave out, and she sank to the floor, gasping for breath. She pressed her hands to her face, her body trembling uncontrollably.

It wasn't real. It couldn't be real.

But deep down, she knew.

It was real.

And no matter where she went, no matter how far she tried to run, the boy would always be there. Watching. Waiting.

Because she couldn't stop this.

Chapter 25: The Unravelling

Days turned into weeks, and Erica's life continued to spiral out of control. The boy's presence was no longer confined to her nightmares or fleeting glimpses in the operating theatre. He was everywhere now, following her like a shadow she couldn't shake.

At work, she would see him standing in the hallway, watching her from a distance. At home, he would appear in the mirror, his reflection staring back at her with those same wide, unblinking eyes. No matter where she went, he was there, silent and patient, waiting for her to acknowledge him.

The stress was unbearable. Erica found herself avoiding sleep, dreading the moment when she would close her eyes and see him again. She withdrew from her colleagues, isolating herself in an attempt to keep the boy's presence at bay. But it didn't help. Nothing helped.

She began to lose track of time, her days blending into one another in a haze of fear and exhaustion. She stopped going to therapy, stopped answering calls from concerned friends. Her world had shrunk to the size of a hospital ward and the small apartment where she lived alone, trapped in a nightmare she couldn't escape.

And all the while, the boy's voice echoed in her mind.

"You can't stop this."

One night, as she sat in her darkened apartment, staring blankly at the wall, Erica felt something shift in the air around her. It was subtle at first, like a change in temperature, but it quickly grew more oppressive. The familiar sensation of being watched settled over her like a weight pressing down on her chest.

Her hands trembled as she stood from the couch, her eyes darting around the room. She could feel him. He was here.

"Stop it," she whispered, her voice hoarse from lack of sleep. "You're not real. You're not."

But deep down, she knew that was a lie.

The boy's voice answered her, soft and cold, as if he were standing right beside her.

"You can't escape."

Erica spun around, her heart pounding in her chest, but the room was empty.

And then she saw him.

Standing in the doorway to her bedroom, his small frame illuminated by the faint glow of the streetlight outside. His wide eyes bore into hers, unblinking, unwavering.

Erica's breath caught in her throat as she backed away, her legs weak with terror. She couldn't do this anymore. She couldn't keep living like this—haunted by a boy who wasn't supposed to exist, tormented by a past she couldn't outrun.

Tears welled up in her eyes as she sank to the floor, her back pressed against the cold wall of her apartment.

"Please," she whispered, her voice broken. "Just leave me alone."

But the boy only stared, his expression unchanged.

"You can't stop this," he whispered, his voice echoing through the empty room.

And then, for the first time, he smiled.

A cold, empty smile that sent a shiver down Erica's spine.

The room seemed to darken, the air growing heavier, suffocating her as the boy took a step closer. Erica squeezed her eyes shut, her body trembling with fear.

And when she opened them again, the boy was gone.

But his voice remained, echoing in the corners of her mind, a constant reminder of the darkness that followed her wherever she went.

"You can't stop this."

And deep down, Erica knew he was right.

There was no escape.

Not for her.

Not anyone

Chapter 26: The Descent

Erica felt like she was living in a nightmare from which she couldn't wake up. The boy's haunting presence had taken over her life, slipping into every corner of her existence. Her waking moments were consumed by the fear of seeing him, and in the brief moments when she managed to close her eyes, he would be there, waiting in the shadows of her dreams.

She stopped going to work altogether. The hospital, once a place of order and routine, now felt like a twisted maze where the boy could appear at any moment. Her supervisor had called several times, at first with concern, and then with a stern warning about her absences, but Erica couldn't bring herself to care.

She didn't have the strength to explain what was happening to her—how could she?

The boy was always there.

The few times she left her apartment, it was in a daze. She would walk the streets, trying to lose herself in the crowds, hoping that being surrounded by people would make the boy disappear. But it never worked. No matter how far she wandered, no matter how many faces she passed, she would always see him—just out of sight, standing at the edge of the crowd, watching her with those same wide, sad eyes.

It was as if the boy had become a part of her, an inseparable force that haunted her every step. She couldn't escape him, because he wasn't just following her.

He was inside her mind.

One evening, after hours of pacing her small apartment, Erica finally broke. She stood in the middle of her living room, her hands clenched into fists, her breath coming in short, ragged gasps.

"I'm done!" she screamed, her voice echoing off the walls. "Do you hear me? I can't take it anymore!"

Her words hung in the air, but the apartment remained silent. She waited, her chest heaving, her heart pounding in her ears. But there was no response.

For the first time in what felt like weeks, the oppressive weight of the boy's presence seemed to lift, if only for a moment. The apartment felt empty again. It was a small relief, but Erica grabbed onto it with everything she had. Maybe, finally, it was over. Maybe she had driven him away.

She stumbled to the kitchen, her hands shaking as she reached for a glass of water. She leaned against the counter, trying to calm her racing pulse, willing herself to believe that it was over. That she could move on.

But then she saw the glass.

In the reflection of the water, distorted and faint, she saw him.

The boy.

Standing right behind her.

Erica dropped the glass, her hands flying to her mouth as she gasped. The glass shattered on the floor, but she barely registered the sound. She spun around, her eyes wide, but the boy wasn't there.

It was just her.

Alone.

Her body trembled as she slid to the floor, her back pressed against the cold cabinets, tears streaming down her face. She couldn't live like this. She couldn't keep seeing him, hearing his voice in every shadow, feeling his eyes on her wherever she went.

There had to be a way out. There had to be a way to make it stop.

Erica's breath hitched as a desperate thought entered her mind.

What if this wasn't about her? What if this was about Thomas? About what he had done?

The boy had haunted Thomas before his death. Erica knew that much. She had heard him talk about it during the trial, though no one had taken his ramblings seriously. They had written it off as guilt or insanity, the delusions of a killer who had lost his grip on reality.

But what if Thomas had been right?

What if the boy was real?

Chapter 27: The Investigation

Erica knew she couldn't handle this on her own. She needed answers, and she knew there was only one place to start. She would have to revisit the case—revisit Thomas Greene's dark, twisted history. Maybe there, buried in the details of his crimes, she could find something that would explain why the boy wouldn't leave her alone.

The next morning, she dragged herself to the public library, her body weak from exhaustion. She hadn't slept more than a few hours in the past week, but the burning need for answers pushed her forward. She couldn't live like this anymore—she needed to know why this was happening, why the boy had chosen her.

The library was quiet, almost eerily so. Erica moved through the rows of books, her fingers brushing against the spines as she made her way to the archive section. The articles about Thomas Greene, the "Theatre Killer," had been filed away, buried among other high-profile cases that had rocked the city over the years.

Erica sat down at one of the dusty desks, pulling out the thick file that detailed Thomas's life, his crimes, and his eventual capture. The headlines from that time felt distant, like they belonged to someone else's story.

But now, they felt uncomfortably close.

As she sifted through the newspaper clippings and case reports, she found herself pausing on a detail she had nearly forgotten—something she hadn't paid much attention to during the trial.

Thomas had been obsessed with control. He had used his access to anaesthetic drugs to incapacitate his victims, rendering them powerless under his hands. He had spoken about it openly during his police interviews, admitting that it wasn't the killing itself that drove him—it was the control. The ability to make life and death decisions without interference.

But what Erica had missed before was the connection to the boy.

One of the earliest victims had been a young boy—unidentified at the time. No family had come forward, and no one had been able to trace his identity. The boy had been Thomas's first documented victim, and from what Erica could tell, his most experimental kill. The reports described it as a "curiosity-driven dissection," with Thomas using the boy's unconscious body to test the limits of anaesthesia.

That boy had been left nameless, his body discarded in a way that had barely made the news at the time. His death had been a footnote in Thomas Greene's eventual rise to infamy.

But it hadn't been forgotten.

Not by the boy.

Erica's hands trembled as she stared at the boy's description. It matched perfectly with the one who had been haunting her—the same wide eyes, the same pale face, the same tragic, sad expression.

This was him. The boy.

Thomas's first victim.

The one who had never been named. Never been acknowledged.

Erica's pulse raced as the pieces of the puzzle started to fall into place. The boy wasn't haunting her by accident. He wasn't just some figment of her imagination, born from the trauma of what Thomas had done.

The boy had been real. And now, he was seeking justice—or maybe revenge—for what had happened to him.

He had haunted Thomas in his final days, and now he had turned his attention to her. But why?

Erica pushed back from the desk, her heart hammering in her chest. She needed to know more. There had to be something—some clue that would explain why the boy had latched onto her, why he wouldn't let her go.

As she gathered the clippings, her phone buzzed in her pocket. She pulled it out, her hands still shaking, and saw a new message from an unknown number.

The message contained only four words.

"You can't stop this."

Erica's blood ran cold.

Chapter 28: Confrontation

The message confirmed what Erica had feared all along. The boy was watching her. He was still there, still inside her mind, inside her life.

But this time, she wasn't going to run. She wasn't going to hide.

If the boy wanted her, she would confront him. She had to.

With a renewed sense of determination, Erica left the library and returned to her apartment. She had spent too long running from the fear, too long letting it control her. If she was going to have any chance at a normal life again, she had to face the boy — whatever he was, wherever he came from.

That night, she sat in her living room, the lights dimmed, waiting.

The clock ticked loudly in the silence, each second stretching into an eternity. Erica's hands trembled, but her resolve remained firm. She wasn't going to let him destroy her.

And then, in the corner of the room, she saw him.

The boy.

Standing there, as he always did, his wide eyes fixed on her, his small frame casting a long shadow on the wall.

Erica's breath caught in her throat, but she didn't move.

"You can't stop this," the boy whispered, his voice soft but insistent, like the rustle of leaves in a storm.

Erica stood, her legs shaking, but she held her ground.

"Why are you here?" she demanded, her voice stronger than she felt. "What do you want from me?"

The boy tilted his head slightly, as if considering her question. His expression remained unchanged, but there was something in his eyes — something dark, something hollow.

"You know why," he whispered.

Erica swallowed hard, her heart racing. "You want revenge. For what Thomas did to you."

The boy took a step closer, his bare feet silent on the floor.

"It's not about revenge," he said quietly. "It's about what was taken. I was taken. Forgotten. Left in the dark. And now, so are you."

Erica's chest tightened as the boy's words sank in. She had become part of this darkness, part of the boy's endless, haunting presence. He wasn't going to leave

The boy's voice was like ice, chilling Erica to her core. His words echoed in her mind, each syllable pressing down on her like a weight she couldn't shake off.

"Forgotten… left in the dark… so are you."

She swallowed hard, her throat tight, but she couldn't let herself give in to the fear this time. She had to understand, had to face him fully.

"What do you mean, 'so are you'?" she asked, her voice trembling but steady enough to hold.

The boy took another step closer, his face expressionless yet filled with a strange intensity. His eyes seemed to pierce through her, as if he could see into her soul, into the deepest parts of her that she had tried so hard to bury.

"You were there," he whispered, his voice soft yet carrying the weight of accusation. "You survived, but you were marked."

"Marked?" Erica shook her head, confused. "I don't understand."

The boy's pale face didn't change, but his eyes darkened. "When you escaped Thomas, he left a part of you behind. A part of you that belongs to the darkness now. That's why you can't stop this. That's why I'm here."

Erica's heart pounded in her chest. She wanted to scream, to deny what he was saying, but something deep inside her knew that the boy was telling the truth. She had escaped the horrors of the warehouse that night, but not all of her had made it out. A part of her had been left behind, lost to the same darkness that consumed Thomas Greene.

"No," Erica whispered, shaking her head. "I'm not like him. I didn't do anything wrong. I'm not part of this!"

The boy's sad smile returned, cold and knowing. "You didn't have to do anything. He marked you the moment he chose you."

Tears welled up in Erica's eyes, her body trembling as the truth of the boy's words sank in. Thomas had chosen her, singled her out, and in doing so, he had dragged her into a world of nightmares and shadows. The darkness wasn't just following her—it was inside her now, a part of her that she couldn't escape.

The boy took one last step toward her, close enough now that she could feel the cold air around him, his presence suffocating. His wide eyes locked onto hers, and in them, she saw something she hadn't seen before.

Not just sadness, not just anger.

But longing.

"You can't run from it, Erica," he whispered. "It's time to stop running."

Erica's breath caught in her throat as the boy's words echoed through her mind. She couldn't run from it anymore. She couldn't keep pretending that it wasn't real. The boy wasn't just haunting her out of vengeance—he was trying to bring her into the darkness, to pull her into the same shadowy place where he had been left, forgotten and alone.

She had to make a choice.

She could keep running, keep fighting against the darkness that consumed her, or she could face it head-on. She could confront the shadows, confront the boy, and finally put an end to it all.

With a deep, shaky breath, Erica wiped the tears from her eyes and stood tall. She looked the boy in the eyes, her fear still there but mixed with something else - resolve.

"Tell me what I have to do," she said, her voice steady now, no longer trembling. "Tell me how to stop this."

The boy blinked slowly, his head tilting slightly as if considering her words. For a moment, the air in the room seemed to grow even colder, the shadows lengthening around them, and then he spoke.

"You have to go back," the boy whispered. "You have to finish what he started."

Erica's blood ran cold. "Go back... to the warehouse?"

The boy nodded. "You have to face it. Face him. Only then can you be free."

Her heart raced as the weight of the boy's words settled over her. She had thought she could leave the past behind, that escaping the warehouse meant escaping Thomas's grasp, but she had been wrong. The warehouse was where it had all begun, and it was where it would have to end.

"I... I don't know if I can do that," Erica admitted, her voice faltering.

The boy's expression didn't change, but his voice softened, almost as if he understood her fear. "It's the only way."

Erica closed her eyes for a moment, taking a deep breath as she tried to summon the strength she didn't think she had. She had survived Thomas once — barely — but now she would have to return to the place where her nightmares were born. The idea of going back to that warehouse filled her with dread, but she knew the boy was right.

She couldn't run from this anymore.

When she opened her eyes, the boy was gone.

Chapter 29: Back to the Darkness

The warehouse stood as it had the last time Erica had seen it—cold, crumbling, and full of the shadows that had haunted her for so long. The rain fell steadily as she stood at the entrance, her heart pounding in her chest. This place had been the site of so much horror, so much fear, and now she was returning to face it.

To end it.

Her hands shook as she pushed open the rusted door, the screech of metal echoing in the empty night. The air inside was damp and cold, just as it had been the night Thomas had captured her. The faint smell of decay still lingered in the air, mixing with the dust that had settled over the years.

Every step felt heavier than the last as she made her way through the warehouse, her eyes scanning the dark corners for any sign of movement. The shadows seemed to close in around her, and the oppressive silence was deafening. But Erica forced herself to keep moving.

She couldn't turn back now.

As she reached the center of the warehouse, the place where Thomas had once held her captive, she stopped. Her breath was shallow, her hands trembling, but she didn't run. This was where it had to happen.

This was where it would end.

Suddenly, the air around her seemed to shift, growing colder, heavier, as if the darkness itself had come alive. The shadows on the walls stretched and twisted, and from the corner of her eye, she saw him.

The boy.

He stood at the edge of the room, his wide eyes locked onto hers, just as he always had. But this time, there was something different in his gaze. It wasn't just sadness or anger.

It was expectation.

Erica's pulse raced, but she forced herself to stay calm. "I'm here," she whispered, her voice barely audible. "I came back, just like you said."

The boy didn't move, didn't speak, but his presence seemed to fill the entire room. Erica could feel the weight of his gaze, the weight of the darkness that surrounded him.

"What do I do now?" she asked, her voice trembling despite her best efforts.

For a long moment, there was only silence.

And then, the boy took a step forward.

"You know what you have to do," he whispered.

Erica's breath caught in her throat. She had thought she was ready, thought she understood what it meant to confront the darkness. But now, standing here, face-to-face with the boy, she realized she hadn't fully understood.

The darkness wasn't something she could fight.

It was something she had to accept.

With a shaky breath, Erica stepped forward, closing the distance between herself and the boy. The air around her grew colder, and the shadows seemed to close in tighter, but she didn't stop. She couldn't.

The boy reached out his hand, and Erica hesitated for only a moment before taking it.

As their hands touched, a wave of cold washed over her, and for a split second, she felt as if the entire world had fallen away. The darkness rushed in, enveloping her, pulling her deeper into its depths.

But she didn't fight it.

She let it take her.

And in that moment, Erica understood.

The boy wasn't just haunting her.

He was leading her.

Leading her to the place where the shadows lived, where the darkness had always been. She had been running from it, denying it, but now, finally, she had accepted it.

The boy's voice echoed in her mind, soft and distant.

"You're free now."

And as the darkness consumed her, Erica felt something she hadn't felt in a long time.

Peace.

Epilogue: The Shadows Remain

Months passed, and the stories of Erica's disappearance began to fade. No one knew what had happened to her—some said she had left the city, others whispered that she had lost her mind after surviving the horrors of Thomas Greene.

But those who had known her, those who had worked with her at the hospital, remembered her in quiet moments. They remembered the way she had changed after the trial, the way she had withdrawn, haunted by something none of them could see.

And though they never spoke of it openly, some of them had started to notice strange things around the hospital once again.

The lights in the operating theatres would flicker at odd times.

Tools would go missing, only to be found later in strange places.

And some of the newer staff had reported seeing something—a figure standing just out of sight, watching them from the shadows.

A boy.

Pale, with wide, sad eyes.

But those who had been there, those who remembered, knew better.

It wasn't just the boy anymore.

Now, there were two.

And they were waiting.